WITHDRAWN

Neil's Castle

BY alissa imre geis

VIKING

VIKING

Published by Penguin Group

Penguin Young Readers Group, 345 Hudson Street, New York, New York 10014, U.S.A.

Penguin Books Ltd, 80 Strand, London WC2R 0RL, England

Penguin Books Australia Ltd, 250 Camberwell Road, Camberwell, Victoria 3124, Australia

Penguin Books Canada Ltd, 10 Alcorn Avenue, Toronto, Ontario, Canada M4V 3B2

Penguin Books (N.Z.) Ltd, 182-190 Wairau Road, Auckland 10, New Zealand

First published in 2004 by Viking, a division of Penguin Young Readers Group

1 3 5 7 9 10 8 6 4 2

LIBRARY OF CONGRESS CATALOGING-IN-PUBLICATION DATA

Geis, Alissa Imre.

Neil's castle / by Alissa Imre Geis.

p. cm.

Summary: Neil dreams of a castle and, with his father's help, he finally creates one.

ISBN 0-670-03609-9

[1. Dreams—Fiction. 2. Imagination—Fiction. 3. Castles—Fiction. 4. Fathers and sons—Fiction.] I. Title.

PZ7.G2715Ne 2004   [E]—dc22   2003012328

Manufactured in China

Set in Worchester

Book design by Nancy Brennan

for Nelson

SPECIAL THANKS TO:

mama, papa, stephie, krissy, kurt, liebe oma und opa,

grandma, grandpa, trina & cricket, tori, risd, rupert & miranda,

a pink construction paper heart, anna & mühle der schönen künste, clementines,

allison, nick, susan, david (not henry james), paris, penny, brooklyn, oren, smilla,

sophie & the sandbox, grace, linda, anna, bob, cathy, tracy, brid, stacey & alexander,

lugh, joanne, nessa, denise, nancy, giovanna, big sur, adam, bob, ro, olivia,

and blue blue sky.

eil woke up remembering his dream. He had dreamed of a castle.

At breakfast, Neil couldn't stop thinking about the castle. He remembered standing on the draw-bridge. When he looked up, he saw the tall towers with their pointed tops. When he looked down, he saw little orange fish swimming in the deep moat. Then he walked to the castle gate and went inside. Up a winding staircase, Neil found a room with windows and a chair just his size to sit in.

After breakfast, Neil went outside to his sandbox. He filled buckets with sand to build towers. But the sand was too dry, and the castle was short and lumpy. It didn't have tall towers like in his dream. Then Neil thought of his wooden blocks.

He ran inside and began stacking blocks, one on top of
another. The towers grew tall and the wall circled round.
But the castle was so little that Neil couldn't sit inside
like in his dream.

Neil had an idea. He dragged the chairs from the dining room table into a circle. He covered them with a blanket to make a castle.

But when he climbed inside, it was small and dark. There were no windows and no towers. This wasn't the castle from his dream.

Neil found his father at the drafting table in his studio. Neil watched as his father drew.

Neil picked up a pencil.

"Dad, I want to draw, too."

"All right," said his father. "You know where the paper is."

"No," said Neil. "That paper is too small. I want to draw something that's really big—bigger than me."

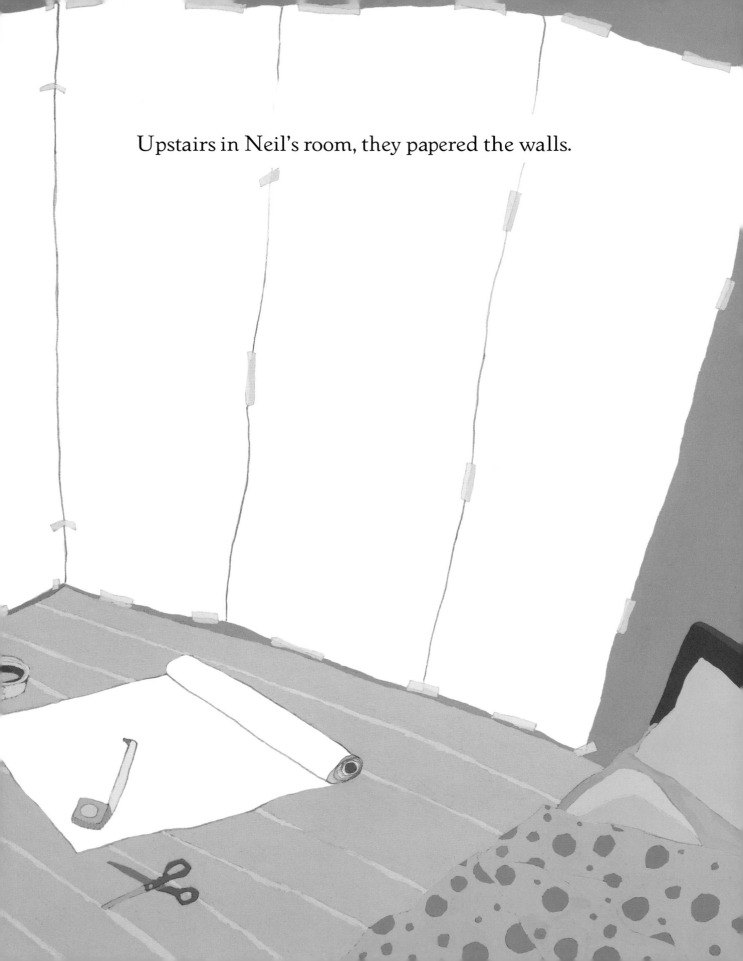

Upstairs in Neil's room, they papered the walls.

Neil began to draw.

He drew

and drew

and drew.

Then he stood back. He looked at what he'd done and thought some more about his dream.

He erased here and here and here.
Then he began to paint.

When Neil stood back again and looked he started
to smile.

"Dad," he called down the stairs. "It's finished."

Neil took his father's hands. "Come and see," he said,
leading his father into the room.

"Here's my castle," Neil said. "I drew it just like the one in my dream. See the drawbridge and the door in the gate? See the tall towers and the staircase?" Neil showed his father the pointed tops of the towers and the little orange fish in the moat.

Neil set two little
chairs in the corner.
"Look, we can sit
inside," he said, and
they sat down.

"This is just like my dream except that you are here, too,"
said Neil, resting his head against his father.

"This is an amazing castle," said his father, and he hugged
Neil close.